A GIRL IN TRAP

A MOMENT HAS CHANGED A GIRL'S LIFE

ROY JUNIOR

“"DEDICATED TO THE ONES WHO LOVE ME"”

Contents

Foreword

No particular foreword just go forward!

Preface

If I give a preface it would be a spoiler so as I don't like spoilers I won't give a one, but I would definitely say that the story would grab your attention!!!

Acknowledgements

I have no problem with this page as it has something to do with;

I thank ***Mr. Ganesh Praneeth Roy Avula a.k.a Roy Junior i.e Myself*** for all my efforts in creating a glory of fiction.

ONE

CHAPTER 1

In the United Kingdom, there lives the Williams family, which includes a girl named Lucy Williams and her grandfather named John Williams. Lucy's father and mother had undergone a mysterious death but this secret is not known by Lucy, it is only known to her grandfather. But he never reveals it to her because if she knows she starts digging deeper into the issue which is harmful to both of them. One day her friends came to her home and started having fun and after some time they got bored and asked Lucy if she had any games. Then she went to the storeroom and searched for any games and she found a CHESSBOARD.

Message from the writer: "From here the story takes a turn so concentrate on every minute

aspect.

Lucy took the Chessboard and took it to her friends. She opened it in front of her friends and everyone saw a warning sign saying "It is a game of kings who are ready to die for their kingdom. Be careful and read every instruction completely and even though you want to play then no one can stop you.

Instructions:

1. Avoid blacks.

2. Try as hard as you can to win the game.

3. There are no draws in the game.

a) If only two kings remain, the one who lost all the other pieces first is the loser.

b) If a stalemate occurs then the opposition candidate wins.

4. The total game including the moves of each player and their surroundings are stored in the form of video, up to the last three games.

5. If anyone tries to harm the chessboard technically or physically, then total data stored till then even the last three games will be lost forever.

6. Never leave the game in the middle.

7. No time limit in this game but the chessboard can understand that you're thinking about your move or trying to escape the game.

8. Don't lose any pieces provided with the board, if the lost board cannot accept another type of pieces and the place will be left empty and the game continues.

9. Whites win games mostly.

10. Face least number checks as possible you can.

Just after reading the first instruction one of Lucy's friend Dannie, who is Afro-American, closed the instruction manual and told Lucy "let's play" and they both started playing. Toss has done traditionally(one of the players keep one black pawn in one hand and white pawn in another hand asks the opponent to choose one hand then opponent plays the colour of the pawn he or she chose.), Dannie was holding the pawns and Lucy chose the right hand which had a white pawn in it. Both of them thought that it was Lucy's luck and moved forward. Chessboard said, "The Game Starts Now" in a bold voice. They started the match, as usual, Lucy started the game with the Queen's Gambit pawn opening(it is the most common opening of normal chess players in which they need to sacrifice a pawn to open many chances to the Queen.). Then Dannie who is a state player in chess and he knows that Sicilian Defence(in

which the black first moves the pawn in front of the queen's bishop) is the best defence for a black player against Queen's Gambit. The Sicilian Defence is a chess opening that begins with the following moves: 1. e4 c5 The Sicilian is the most popular and best-scoring response to White's first move 1.e4. Opening 1.d4 is a statistically more successful opening for White because of the high success rate of the Sicilian defence against 1.e4(Queen's Gambit). But he started playing king's pawn opening which may lead to checkmate in the next two moves. Lucy looked strangely at Dannie thinking that what happened to his mind had he lost it, and

played further and she won the game by checkmate. It is considered a very foolish opening in chess history and no chance of escaping from a checkmate. So no one would like to play it but unfortunately, Dannie played it. After the game Chessboard said, "Lucy won

the game and Dannie lost". All of them were shocked that how could a game board know our names? Lucy was happy that she won against a state player in chess and celebrated the moment with her friends. But Dannie was thinking how could I play such a foolish game against Queen's Gambit and went home. Lucy was getting interested in playing chess and went to Dannie's house to learn some tactics in chess, but when she entered his house with a

smile, what she saw was gloomy scenery and asked Dannie's mother what is the reason for this silence, she replied that Dannie had undergone a death sentence due to some foul behaviour at Queen's palace. Lucy was in shock and went to John Williams to tell about this. When she said this, John told her that you have to forget some sad and bad things in your life and to do it you have to enjoy yourself, so go and play with your friends. Lucy went to her bedroom and cried for hours and thought that anything which happens under the law is correct for everyone and thought that what happened to Dannie might be right and called her friends to play chess and have fun tonight. Lucy's friends came to her house and started having fun and one of them told Lucy "You think you are a champ by defeating Dannie if you then come and defeat me", she didn't take it as a challenge and thought it would be a time pass. This time Lucy was the one holding pawns and her friend Lara was the one to choose and Lara chose black, Lara said "lucky girl got white", Lucy replied if you want white you can take it but

Lara refused and said let's play professionally, Chessboard said, " No you cannot exchange colours after a traditional toss". Chessboard said, "The game starts now". They started playing, this time Lucy played Blackmar-Diemer Gambit(which is also one the most successful openings for white, it is the same as Queen's Gambit but here we move first the king's pawn two steps forward instead of Queen's pawn). Lara thought that this was an easy game with Vienna Defence(it is the best defence against Blackmar-Diemer Gambit), but she started with the Sicilian defence which doesn't work better for Blackmar-Diemer Gambit, Lucy was laughing inside and saw Lara, Lara was smiling awkwardly, then Lucy thought that she might have fallen into Lara's trap and was concentrating on the game. Finally, Lucy gave a check to Lara's king with the

Knight and made a checkmate with her pawn. Lara was in a blow that how

she could play that stupid at Lucy's Blackmar-Diemer Gambit. And Lara told her friends that there is something wrong with the Chessboard because every time Lucy gets white and she wins the match with opponents foolish play, nobody cares about Lara's words and they said, "loser always tries to defend his or her own mistakes". Lara went home late because she was hit by a horse on the street. Lara was not that close to her friends that they could communicate with each other staying at different places. Lara died after two days of play, due to trespassing the military wall one of the military soldiers shot her in the head; she died on the spot. Her body was given to her family and the funeral happened a week after the death but no one of her friends had attended the funeral and not even cremation. Lara's parents were very hurt that no one of her friends had attended the funeral and cremation, so they went to Lucy's home and had an exchange of words and told Lucy's that "Lara died a week ago and no one came to her funeral and cremation". By hearing this Lucy was undergoing insomnia(sleeplessness) and prescribed to use sleeping pills to have a good sleep and rest. She was addicted to sleeping pills and took more than prescribed, this was noticed by her

grandfather John Williams and admitted her to a rehabilitation centre for treatment. After a week she was good without pills and her insomnia was gone. This time also her grandfather told her the same thing when Dannie died but she couldn't recognise that and invited her friends again this time she won against two of her friends by playing white. The next day both of them died of the same cause and at the same place and at the same time as they were together. They died because a group of elephants were running on Royal Street at the same time they were on the street, even though they tried to escape but they couldn't escape the Herd and died due to a stampede. This news came to Lucy's notice, she now understands that all this is not a natural thing and it is suspicious. And went to Royal street to know actually what happened that day but she found everything quite natural at the crime scene. She started an investigation into these suspicious deaths and she was investigating first Dannie's case and found that he died of a Death sentence given by the Queen. She went home and opened

the chessboard and started reading the instructions given in it. When she was reading the 3.a and 3.b instructions she became nervous and thinking that why there would be no draw and what happens to the loser, then she read the 4th instruction and got angry with herself and started searching game video of Dannie but she couldn't find it as it was last 4th game and as usual the chessboard erased it. But without reading the 5th instruction she went to a nearby hacker and asked him to restore the previous file but as a result of technical harm total data was lost and the hacker couldn't do anything to restore it. Then she was trying to think of the game she played with Dannie but couldn't get anything, again and again, she tried as hard as she could and finally, she got something important that she made a checkmate with the queen and the reason for the death of Dannie is also Queen. But she thought it may be a coincidence and made research on Lara's death and found that the day she played a game with Lara she got hurt by the horse and she died due to a soldier. Now she started thinking about the game she played with Lara and found something very suspicious. She made a check with the Knight and then a checkmate with a pawn the same as Lara's death, first hit by a horse and died by a military soldier. She was very nervous that she was also one of the reasons for their deaths as she was the one who bought the chessboard into their lives and became a murderer. So she tried to break it but nothing happened. She went to her grandfather and asked about the

chessboard, who invented it and why it was in our storeroom because of that four of my friends died. Then his grandfather just gave her a warning that "avoid it as much as you can as it won't avoid you as you opened it after a long time". Then Lucy asked John Williams "how could I get white four times and win all four games without having any professional knowledge about the game." John Williams replied, "THE MYSTERIOUS CHESSBOARD had chosen you as its white King who is the leader of all other pieces and it wants the white King to never lose and it always provides white to you in any kind of toss and it also influences the opponent's mind to play foolishly against you because you have to win the game". Lucy told John Williams to stay there, I will read all the instructions and come here again. Lucy went to the chessboard and read all the instructions and returned to John Williams and said that in instructions, nowhere it is mentioned that the loser dies then John replied, "didn't you focus on the second, third and tenth instructions, each of these institutions has some meaning, let me explain to you. The second one(Try as hard as you can to win the game) means to try to save your life indirectly. The third one(There are no draws in the game) means any one of you must die after the game. The tenth one(Face least number checks as possible you can) means the number of checks you face in the game are the number of problems you face before you die. "How can say that fluently about the instructions even without seeing them and how many time did you play it and how many times you became the reason of deaths," asked Lucy to John Williams, then he replied, "I played it twenty-seven times", Lucy

said, " you are still alive it means all other twenty-seven are dead now right?", John Williams said "yes", Lucy again asked, "Why did this time THE MYSTERIOUS

CHESSBOARD chose you as its white king", John Williams left without answering Lucy's question.

Lucy went out in search of her grandfather John Williams and at last, she found him at the lake

Windermere, sitting on a stone and watching the lake. Lucy asked him "why did you leave like that without answering me?"John said, " it would be good for us without answering it and just leave it". Lucy went back home and started searching for any information related to the chessboard but she found nothing. Then she went to a nearby library to know the history of THE MYSTERIOUS CHESSBOARD, there she found a book named "Untold facts about THE MYSTERIOUS CHESSBOARD", then she started reading it, after reading it, she had all the knowledge about that chessboard. In that book, it was written that THE MYSTERIOUS CHESS BOARD was invented by Franklin James, but no one knows what happened to him. But she went home and asked John Williams Who was Franklin James but John said he didn't know about him. She went to the storeroom and searched thoroughly and found some photos of her grandfather John Williams but she ignored them and searching for related items but she found something like a key, while she dusting the key she misplaced it and while searching it on the floor she saw a name written with the small font on the corner of the photos, she brought her magnifying glass and looked carefully at the name. It was "Franklin James", she was stunned looking at it. She ran to her grandfather who was at the lake but this time he wasn't there. She was trying to find him but she couldn't so she went home and had a horrible sleep. The next day in the news "Missing Franklin James found dead in the lake Windermere". Lucy felt very lonely because John Williams alias Franklin James was the only one who was looking after her but now no one is there to look after her. She thought that my grandfather would leave me something I wanted and went to the lake and started searching in and around the lake. She found a toolbox but it was inside the crime scene so she couldn't take it and go. So she bought a new toolbox and replaced it. She took it home and opened it, she saw a similar key which she found in the storeroom. Then she made a research on the keys like that and what they meant for, in her research, she noticed that there are no locks that can be opened through these keys and these are not keys at all.

Then, Lucy thought, "then what are these keys meant for?", she opened the chessboard and saw everything she could find in it, then she saw a groove where these key-like items can fit. She inserted one of them into the groove then the chessboard said, "Lucy you became the permanent white king of me but I have another key if you have it insert in or keep it secretly

with you because if someone inserts they would become the permanent white king of me and there is no other option to me". Lucy asked the chessboard "why you want only me as your white king and why not others". Chessboard replied, "because Lucy, you are the only one who cared about others lives and worked for it till now thirty-one games have been played in four of them are played by you and twenty-seven of them were played by you grandfather, but he never thought about his opponents in which two of them were your father and mother and one more thing you played without knowing the consequences but he played by knowing them, in

fact, he invented me". Lucy was shocked that her parents were killed by her grandfather. After some time she woke up and asked the chessboard how a man could create something which creates a machine that brings a natural death to humans. Chessboard replied, "I was a normal human being who had a job at the library, but one day my friends called me to play chess in a competition for money. In that competition, the finals were between me and Franklin James. According to the rules, he won the match, I accept that but my friends who needed money very badly refused to accept that and they complained about the competition that Franklin James had cheated the game to win and he was disqualified by the authorities." Then what happened next asked Lucy, chessboard replied, "After a week I felt very bad about what happened to Franklin James and went to him and said to apologise me for my mistake but in return, he cursed me that I would become the killer of many lives who plays chess, that curse turned me like this. In that twenty-five, excluding your parents, four of them were my friends, think once how could I feel." Lucy replied, "For every problem, there is a solution and your problem too would have a solution, let's find it and why didn't you mentioned death clearly in

the instructions", the chessboard replied, "Instructions were written by Franklin James, not by me". Lucy inquired chessboard that where were you originated, Chessboard replied, "In the Windermere lake", Now Lucy is getting everything in clarity and she took the chessboard and went to lake Windermere and again asked, "where were you exactly originated inside or on the shore", Chessboard replied, "I originated inside the lake and by the way, call me Tommy, it's my name." She dove into the lake without hesitation and searched all the lake and ultimately she found something related to the chessboard, it was a cryptex which was carved with all the symbols of chess pieces. But she doesn't know the code to open it. It will open when only a six-digit correct passcode is entered, if we try to open it by force the secret scroll inside it will get burnt. She tried all the combinations related to chess and its pieces but none of them worked out. She asked Tommy, alias THE MYSTERIOUS CHESSBOARD, that he might know something related to it but he doesn't have any idea about it. Then she took it to a worker at Queen's palace who had an outstanding knowledge about the history and was a grandmaster, ultimately he also failed in opening the cryptex. Then she took an appointment to meet the Queen and discuss this. Her appointment was approved as she was the only one who was investigating these unknown linked natural deaths in which one of them involved the Queen. The next day she met the Queen at the Palace. Then Lucy inquired Queen about THE

MYSTERIOUS CHESSBOARD whether she knows about it or not, but Queen replied with a shocking answer that she knows about it and her father was the maker of that chessboard and said she had lost her mother due to it. Lucy replied arrogantly "What! it's my grandfather who

made the chessboard, Your Highness sorry for my arrogance at you...",

Queen replied politely that her father was Franklin James and that she also knew that Lucy's grandfather is also Franklin James alias John Williams, then Lucy asked the

Queen to give their family tree so that she could get some clarity on these complicated relationships. Queen provided her family tree and Lucy found that what Queen said about her father and my grandfather was exactly correct. Lucy was totally confused and was helpless. Then she went home and had a break from all this stuff and went back to lake Windermere to reconstruct the crime scene because most of the unsolved cases were solved by reconstructing the crime scene.

After reconstructing the crime scene with the help of the police and forensic team, Lucy and her team re-investigated the entire lake and crime scene, then they came to a stunning conclusion that it was not a suicide and it was pre-planned cold-blooded murder. Lucy was thinking that who might kill my grandfather because he won against twenty-four others excluding my parents and Queen's mom, all the other's family members would have enmity on my grandfather. Lucy with the help of the police started an investigation on the other family members. She found that twenty-one of their families were found unsuspicious and three of them were found suspicious. After the investigation, she went home and had a confusing sleep. When she woke up she went to the storeroom and searched for the lost key-like thing but she couldn't find it. While searching she was roaming all the storeroom but at a place, the sound was different while walking on it. Then she took a hammer and tried to smash it and tried to open it but she couldn't open it, then she went to replace the hammer from where she took it from. When replacing she saw a note written on the wall near the actual location of the hammer that " Every door has a key and to open a door there is no need of strength, it can be opened with intelligence, so go and search for a key, not a better hammer." Lucy was in a concussion that somebody already knew that I would come across that basement door and I would search for the hammer to smash it but who was that somebody. Lucy was in high confidence that somebody was her grandfather John Williams alias, Franklin James. She was searching for a key to open the basement door to open it, but she searched for it not the

only in the storeroom but also the whole house. Again she went to the Queen and asked whether she might know about the key, Queen replied, "No, I don't know about the key about which you are asking about, ok leave it, what about the cryptex, did you crack it." Lucy ran

unanswered quickly to home thinking that cryptex is the only possible solution to find the key. Lucy examined the cryptex very well and found that code to open it can be concluded from the carvings on cryptex. She worked hard on the symbols and logos carved on the cryptex and finally opened it with a passcode that was "CHAMPY", which had the meaning indicating that Franklin James would be a chess champion. After opening it Lucy found a scroll written in the Latin language which she couldn't understand. She went to a Latin translator to translate this information into English. He refused to do so because he said that it is not only in Latin, it is a

combination of Latin and Greek and only one person in the United Kingdom knows these two languages very well, known as "Peaky Blinder" and he is an Indian but lives in the UK since 1980, you can find him at 221 C Baker Street. She went to Peaky Blinder and showed this

scroll and asked him to translate. Then he asked her "What is your name?", she replied, "Lucy". He went inside a room and gave her the key she wanted. She was astonished and asked him " Why did you give me without asking? ", he replied that in the scroll it was written "first ask the name of the person who gave you the scroll if the answer was "Lucy" then give the key I gave youâ€¦ Franklin James". Lucy was happy and thought that her grandfather was a true Grandmaster not only in chess but also in intelligence. Then she took the key and went home to open the basement when she opened it she found.

When Lucy opened the basement door she saw a lot of super computers and a lot of technical stuff and when she opened her phone, she saw that her phone was already connected to the wireless network of the basement and her mobile got hung because of such a high-speed internet, that normal smartphone couldn't handle and she was thinking that then why this wireless network even ever detected by my phone because it has a good speed it might have a good range too but, I never saw my phone detecting it. It means there's some technical barrier between the basement and the rest. She made a trail by holding her phone facing it and as soon as she stepped out of the door that wireless network was disconnected

and as soon as she entered the room the wireless network was connected. Then she confirmed that signal jammers are present, to be safe from hacks to trace Franklin James who might be the key player of this whole mystery. Lucy suddenly thought that what might be the

connection between Franklin James and Peaky Blinder, and she kept this thought aside and started working on the stuff in the supersonic basement room. There she found that Franklin was a hacker because, in that room, Lucy could access all the security cameras of the United

Kingdom, but all the systems in the room could be accessed by her fingerprints. She saw some large frameworks made of synthetic plastic to make them light and she saw a huge box filled with animal skins in the form of leather. She was confused that what could anyone do with this huge amount of leather either sell it or it might be Franklin's passion. She went to 221 C Baker Street to meet Peaky Blinder to know about the connection between him and Franklin James. When she went there she saw Peaky Blinder talking to someone, she knocked on the bench to grab his attention, then Peaky Blinder asked her " Hey, you young lady What do you want now, I already gave what I had which belongs to you!" Lucy said " how did he give you like that and how can he trust someone stranger like you?"Peaky Blinder replied, " You say me a stranger, I am the first child of Franklin James and your dad was the third and I am own brother of the Queen, you might not come across my name in the family tree because I told them to not include me in this complicated relationship". Lucy said, " Even your sister didn't tell me about you when we met in the palace.", Peaky Blinder said, " In fact, she doesn't know it." Lucy said, "Leave it I would get confused by these complex relationships and by the way to whom were you talking when I came here?" Peaky Blinder said, "He is my neighbour and sometimes whenever this old man needs anything he would come to my home and ask me." Then Lucy left Peaky Blinder and came home back and went to the basement and started thinking why would Franklin be a hacker and need access to all the security cameras of the whole United Kingdom. When she was going through the systems she saw that one of the systems has two suspicious files named "Died" and "To die" but the file "To die" was empty and the file "Died" was containing thirty-one files within it and content of each file was in the same pattern which included, name of the person died, time and date of death, cause of death, his or her death certificate and place of death. In these all

the only common point Lucy noticed was, in the cause of death at last of the paragraph it mentioned in the brackets "THE MYSTERIOUS CHESSBOARD", Lucy was thinking that what is the process that happens to someone in the file "To die" and started thinking that how she could know it. Lucy thought that no one would like to play this game with me knowing that they will die after the game but without playing it, I cannot figure it out. Lucy went to the chessboard and read all the instructions thoroughly once again and made a master plan to trap the one who is doing this.

Instructions:

1. Avoid blacks.

2. Try as hard as you can to win the game.

3. There are no draws in the game.

a) If only two kings remain, the one who lost all the other pieces first is the loser.

b) If a stalemate occurs then the opposition candidate wins.

4. The total game including the moves of each player and their surroundings are stored in the form of video, up to the last three games.

5. If anyone tries to harm the chessboard technically or physically, then total data stored till then even the last three games will be lost forever.

6. Never leave the game in the middle.

7. No time limit in this game but the chessboard can understand that you're thinking about your move or trying to escape the game.

8. Don't lose any pieces provided with the board, if the lost board cannot accept another type of pieces and the place will be left empty and the game continues.

9. Whites win games mostly.

10. Face least number checks as possible you can.

Lucy made a human-like robot with stuff in the basement and started playing chess with it and she won the game. As soon as the game completed she saw the game video (instruction number four "The total game including moves of each player their surroundings are stored in

the form of video, up to the last three games.") and she noted all her moves and checks and checkmate moves in her mind and she never left the robot alone. Once she went to the basement to check whether the robot name is included in the " To die " file or not but when she saw the list robot name was there for few seconds and the list updated automatically and showed the list is empty and she was terrified and searched in " Died " file weather robot name included or not but when she saw it, robot name was there in the list and time of death was a minute ago and place of death was Lucy's house and cause of death was "Camel stamping(THE MYSTERIOUS CHESSBOARD)". She ran upstairs and saw the dead robot. Lucy was in shock that how could someone come into my home and kill like that, that too in a fraction of seconds and all the scenarios were the same as the game. Nothing was there except the footprints left all over the house. Lucy thought how could all these happen this

fast and no evidence is left to prove except those footprints. Then she got an idea and started examining the footprints and she compared them with the other footprints of the same animal but they weren't matched. Then she went to the basement and saw the huge frameworks and noticed that some were missing and felt that these are not real animals, these are just robots.

But who is assembling them this fast as soon as the game completes and how could someone know that the game has been played because only me and Tommy(THE MYSTERIOUS CHESSBOARD) knows about it. It means Tommy is the one leaking the information, but to whom. She asked Tommy "why are you doing this?" Tommy replied, "I told you it's my curse and duty to do It.", Lucy asked Tommy "To whom did you inform", Tommy replied " If I answer this question it would be against my rules if I cross my rules I would remain like this forever if I won't I would become a human again ", Lucy, went to the Chess championship authority and inquired about Tommy and Franklin match but what they said was that not even a name Tommy registered on that tournament and Franklin James was the champion of that tournament. Lucy had a dreadful time with all the lies around her and she took a nap and got ready to interrogate Tommy alias THE MYSTERIOUS CHESSBOARD, Lucy took the chessboard to the heating furnace and asked to tell me all the truth about all drama that happened till now or else she would throw it into the furnace. Tommy said that his name was really Tommy but the story he told her was a lie, then Lucy asked him " then who are you?". A stunning answer was given by Tommy that he is an AI(Artificial Intelligence) made by Franklin James. Lucy told Tommy " Ok now tell me the truth, what is happening here?" Tommy said, "Why would I tell you because after that you would throw me in the furnace, ok throw me but after that, your mystery gets solved!?" Lucy left to the police department and asked for security camera footage of the Royal Street of the day her friends died then she noticed there three elephants more than usual and they look odd, this confirmed that these deaths are not natural, and these are murders and they must be investigated and the culprit must be punished for his crimes. Lucy went home and went down to the basement and thought that she wasted time on requesting the footage as I could see it from here but it would be illegal. She then tried to retrace the culprit who was accessing these systems from elsewhere and killing innocents. But she couldn't find anything about the culprit. Then she took one of the systems out of the basement and again tried to retrace because inside the basement there are signal jammers again also she failed to trace the culprit. Then Lucy asked the police about the progress of the investigation but they said "just leave solid evidence, culprit not even left a clue except the false footprints with which we couldn't get anything". She went to meet the Queen and told her about Peaky Blinder that he is Queen's own brother. Queen recollected about the words her mother said about her brother in childhood "he was a psycho so that we left him alone but your father(Franklin James) didn't like it". Listening to the Queen's words Lucy left the palace and drove to 221 C Baker Street to meet Peaky Blinder but this time she was too late that his neighbours told her that he left the country an hour ago. Lucy inquired his neighbours about who was the old man she saw with him on the day she met him for the first time. In her inquiry, it was proven that the old man was his father and they would play chess daily, both of them have a great knowledge of chess and every match between them would be interesting to us to watch. Lucy thought "Franklin James is still alive as they said that the old man was Peaky Blinder's father. It means Franklin James alias, John Williams". So she went to the police department and asked permission to dig out her grandfather's dead body to recheck if it is a real one or a fake one, she was very sure that it would be a fake one.

Her assumption was proved wrong by digging out the casket(coffin) as the body was real. Lucy was thinking about who might be the old man. She requested DNA testing on the body they dug out to

confirm that it is Franklin James's body to the forensic team.

Lucy was shocked with the report as the report was positive indicating that the body they found belongs to Franklin James. Lucy was thinking that who might be the old man who was proved as Franklin James? She went to the embassy and inquired about Peaky Blinder and the old man, they gave the details of them. In those details, the name of the old man was

Franklin James, then she asked for his passport details, they provided it immediately as Lucy had special permission of The Queen, in the passport the name was the same, then she argued how can you send someone dead according to the government. They said that he

had passed all the security checks done by them. Lucy was thinking about how it could be possible when someone is dead. There might only be one possibility that there might be two Franklins and they must be monozygotic twins which means they look like exact copies and their DNA will be hundred percent identical. Lucy was thinking " if my assumption is right then why did it not mentioned in the family tree of the Royal family and if they were two to whom my dad was born and to whom Queen was born and to whom

Peaky Blinder was born, but this is not the case right, I have to find them(Franklin James and Peaky Blinder and Franklin James) to know the truth. Lucy flew to Australia, to where they both flew. Now Lucy has to search for them. But she doesn't have as many permissions as she had in the

United Kingdom. Even though she had to find them to put an end to this illegal drama and know the truth. She tried her level best, but couldn't find anything. Then she went

to Bondi Beach to relax for a while. There she saw there was a crowd grouped around something, she went there and she saw a dead body died due to horse stampings and then she reported the Australian police. Lucy thought that it would be planned by them. She asked the police department to let her know if any deaths were reported due to horses, elephants, camels, soldiers and any monarchs like kings and queens. Initially, they refused to give her what Lucy wanted but when she organised a meeting with The Queen they got convinced and gave her what she wanted. Lucy started the investigation by the reports given by Australian police and eventually, she found Peaky Blinder and Franklin James at Hotel The

Langham Melbourne in Melbourne, then she pointed a gun towards Peaky Blinder's head and asked Franklin James to say the truth, then Peaky Blinder said that he cannot answer some inhuman new questions, then Lucy asked Peaky Blinder that if he had any mental issue, Peaky Blinder replied "He doesn't have any and he cannot have such because he is not human, he is an AI robot made by Franklin James. Lucy was in shock and she asked Peaky Blinder "who was the culprit doing all these? is it you?" Then he replied that it wasn't him it was The AI programmed by Franklin James to do all these even in his absence. Lucy asked Peaky Blinder "How were deaths occurring in the same pattern in Australia even though the chessboard was with me." Peaky Blinder replied, " You have one, I have one, rest of the world has seven and you could never reach them out even though you reach you cannot prove them out and by the way my real name is Praneeth Roy and I am not a psycho likewise my family told you " Lucy left Peaky Blinder with full of happiness and a smile on her face. Roy alias Peaky Blinder was confused as to why Lucy left full of happiness and a smile on her face, out of curiosity, Roy went to the airport to meet her and clarify all his doubts. When Roy asked Lucy "why did she leave with happiness instead of tears and had a smile on her face instead of a hurtful face, her answer amazed Roy. Lucy's answer was " You are a son of Franklin James but I am the granddaughter of Franklin James, Don't I deserve to complete his dreams about these chessboards ", Roy asked Lucy "When did you swap to my side? What made you turn this side? Lucy answered " The day you gave me the key to the basement door. When I opened the basement door and stepped in there was an automated message playing from Franklin James saying all about these chess boards and why they were created and why he killed all the twenty-seven members including my parents and Queen's mother. And all the evidence is in the systems. At last, he said the list "To Die" will automatically get updated as soon as you meet Roy in Australia and come back with him and never forget that he is no less than a father for you even compared to your father he is far better...(dove into the lake

Windermere and left his last breath.) Roy packed his bags to return to the United Kingdom for the next flight. They returned to the United Kingdom and had a chat to know each other very well as the next deaths are going to be done together. Lucy took Roy to the basement and showed him all the stuff but Roy wasn't surprised and searched around for something. Lucy asked Roy that why did he not amazed and what he was searching for, Roy said "This is not even one percent of Franklin James recreation and I am searching for the painting of Franklin James in which latitude and longitude of the location to which we have to go to see the real creation of Franklin James are printed in the micro font" Lucy ran upstairs to the storeroom and bought the painting what Roy wanted by seeing Roy asked her a magnifying glass to see the location details and after getting the details of the location, they drove to that location and they saw a huge building with a modern look and they went to the entrance and they heard an automated voice message saying "Lucy and Praneeth Roy, you both can enter this building without hesitation and there will be no security check for both of you as Franklin James instructed." They entered and while seeing all the stuff this time Lucy got surprised and Praneeth Roy already saw twice with his father so no amazement in him. Lucy was enjoying all luxuries in that building and Roy was reading all the articles written by Franklin James and he also noted down the names of the persons to die. Roy went to Lucy and said, "You had enough rest, let's take down the culprits of the society". Lucy replied lazily " Let's start from tomorrow morning..." Roy said "Ok but tomorrow morning at 6 'o'clock. Lucy woke up at 5:30 AM and woke Roy but she saw Roy laying dead on his bed. When she saw it she asked her computer assistant to play the camera footage to know what happened but the assistant replied: " No need of the footage, I killed him by the order of Franklin James ". Lucy asked the assistant that when he had given you order to kill Roy, Assistant replied that he gave me today at 4 AM, while Lucy asking the computer that how could it even possible..Franklin James entered the scene and said " it is possible because I am still alive ". Lucy asked Franklin James " Grandpa then what about the DNA report " Franklin replied " Did you forget that I am a professional hacker, "

Lucy asked James " Why did you kill Roy? ". Franklin James answered, " Can't you see unnatural humbleness in him which leads to very bad scenes?" Lucy told Franklin that he should promise her that he would never leave her alone until his last breath and Franklin agreed on that. Lucy pointed the gun on Franklin's head and said that not to move, Franklin asked " why are you doing this to me?"

Lucy answered "Now I saw unnatural humbleness in you so you have to die" and she shot on his head noticed that it was a robot, after few minutes the voice of Franklin James was heard by Lucy saying that " Good work keep it up, I am with you anytime, anywhere and it's a mystery to you that I am dead or alive and don't waste time on

this question and by the way Roy is not dead it was just a creation of a scene " Lucy was happy to hear that and started

enjoying the deaths of society culprits with her brother Praneeth Roy alias Peaky Blinder.

Message from the writer: "This story may be completed temporarily but a sequential book may be published further, thanks for reading, bye...

TWO

CHAPTER 2

To be Continued in the next part...

9 798886 298741

Printed by Libri Plureos GmbH in Hamburg, Germany